Rail Trail Kitten

Reading is Fun!
Donna M. Ferguson

Written and Illustrated by:
Donna M. Ferguson

ISBN: 1479199516
ISBN 13: 9781479199518

Dedication

**Love to Alexa, Laila, Amina,
and especially to Skip**

Stepping from rail to rail, looking from right to left,
Rail Trail Kitten searches for a home.
"A house, a house, I need a house. Who can help
me find a house?"
He asks his animal friends to help him.

Rail Trail Kitten meets proud Red Rooster.
"Red Rooster, Red Rooster, may I live in your house?"

"My house is made of wood and wire. You will be cold and wet because the wind and rain blow through my house."

Rail Trail Kitten meets frisky Gray Squirrel.

"Gray Squirrel, Gray Squirrel, may I live in your house?"
"My house is high in a tree. You cannot climb that high to my house."

Rail Trail Kitten meets tiny Brown Mouse.
"Brown Mouse, Brown Mouse, may I live in your
house?"

"My house is a hole in the ground. You are too big to squeeze into my house."

Rail Trail Kitten meets fluffy White Rabbit.
"White Rabbit, White Rabbit, may I live in your house?"

"My house is filled with bouncing baby bunnies.
There is no room in my house."

Rail Trail Kitten meets chirping Bluebird."
"Bluebird, Bluebird, may I live in your house?"

"My house is a nest made of twigs and yarn. It is not strong. You will break my house."

Rail Trail Kitten meets leggy Green Frog.
"Green Frog, Green Frog, may I live in your house?"

"My house is beside the water. You will get wet in my house."

Rail Trail Kitten meets fluttering Yellow Butterfly.
"Yellow Butterfly, Yellow Butterfly, may I live in your
house?"

14

"I fly from flower to flower. I do not have a house."

Homeless, Rail Trail Kitten lies down along the trail. He falls asleep until …

"Ding, ding, ding," a bell wakes him.

Rail Trail Kitten sees chubby cheeked Alexa riding
her bike.
"Alexa, Alexa, may I live in your house?"

"Yes, my house is perfect for you. My house needs a kitten."

"Hop in my bike basket."

"Ding, ding, ding, passing on the left," calls chubby cheeked Alexa.

Every day chubby cheeked Alexa and Rail Trail Kitten wave as they ride past proud Red Rooster, frisky Gray Squirrel, tiny Brown Mouse, fluffy White Rabbit, chirping Bluebird, leggy Green Frog, and fluttering Yellow Butterfly.

"Ding, ding, ding, passing on the left," sing chubby cheeked Alexa and Rail Trail Kitten as they ride home.